Broken Pieces

What Binds Us Makes

Invaluable

Broken Pieces

What Binds Us Makes

Invaluable

Abigail Hudson

Edited by

Dr. Ruth Baskerville

Williams and King Publishers

ISBN: 979-8-9851466-46

This book was published as a collaborative effort with the Central Florida Writers and Publishers Guild (a nonprofit organization), So You Want Your Name in Lights (a nonprofit organization), and Williams and King Publishers.

Printed in the USA

Author Contact information:
GivesJoy@gmail.com

Introduction

I wrote this book to remind people that you don't have to conform or change yourself to fit in with people you don't belong with. Be you! People who are true friends will love you and accept you for who you are.

Abigail Hudson

Chapter 1
Elizabeth

I want to introduce you to a girl named Elizabeth. She is sixteen years old and in high school. She's an "A" or "B" student, so she's considered pretty smart. She's not what we might call popular, but she hangs around a group of friends who are close to each other.

Elizabeth is an average-looking girl, and for the most part, she's a giving person. When her friends need someone to talk to, they know Elizabeth is confidential and willing to listen. However, she is not as willing to share her deepest feelings because she's an introvert at heart. Yes, she can be very outgoing, but deep inside, she's a quiet soul. She attends a large public school in the city, and she's active in sports and the performing arts. Elizabeth has a philosophy that while everything is free, this is the perfect time to explore the range of her talents, and to discover what she may want to do in life after high school. Even if she doesn't find a career, she's happy to be a high school kid involved in the life of her school. Also, she works a few hours a week at a *Starbucks* near the school.

Elizabeth is the oldest child of three, and the only girl. Her brothers are nine and ten years old, respectively. They are the typical younger brothers, always trying to get into her business, running to the parents with half-truths, and generally being annoying. Alexander is the ten-year-old brother, and Isaiah is her nine-year-old brother.

Like most teens, Elizabeth sees her brothers as one big unit of tiresome trouble. Her world is far from their immature existence, and she lets them know it often. When she's in her room having a private conversation on her phone, they enter without knocking, and begin giggling and pointing at her. She can be heard daily saying, "Leave me alone, you bothersome bunch!" This comment is guaranteed to incite her little brothers to irritate her more. They stand and fold their hands as if to say, "We're not leaving." Elizabeth always ends up calling her mother for help.

Elizabeth's relationship with her Mom, Jon Marie, is OK. She doesn't share every thought she has, but at the same time, she knows she can count on her Mom to have her back. Her Mom is always ready to listen to what Elizabeth chooses to share with her. Jon Marie works every day at a supermarket where she is the supervisor of the cashiers. She was smart enough to go to college and got as far as her sophomore year before she met and married her husband. Like so many of us, she promised herself that she would finish college, but never did go back. Instead, she had Elizabeth and her two brothers.

Elizabeth's Dad, George, had grown up middle-class, and his parents had to sacrifice to send him to college. Nevertheless, he studied hard and after college and medical school, he became a Neurologist. He had fallen in love with Jon Marie while in undergraduate school, and while he was certainly happy to have fathered three children, he wished that his wife was able to finish college and get a high-paying job. Their marriage was strained after seventeen years, and finally, they got a divorce with the arrangement that the three kids would spend one week with Jon Marie and one week with George, regardless of whether or not school was in session.

Elizabeth wants to live with her Mom, even though she would not mind visiting her Dad. George lives in a mansion in the city, while Jon Marie lives in an apartment closer to her school. She really hates packing up her clothes and belongings every weekend because it's Dad's week or Mom's week.

She isn't very close to her Dad in comparison to her Mom. Whenever she has an issue or needs something, he just says, "Here is the money," or "Google it." That was it. There's no "Let me try to help" or "Let's talk about it."

But to Elizabeth, money and *Google* do not solve all problems. "I like the fact my Dad gives me money, but

4

I just wish he cared more. On the other hand, if one of my brothers throws a fit for no reason, he all of the sudden wants to ask them, '*What is wrong, Buddy?*' followed by a hug or the words, 'Do you need something to eat?"

Elizabeth feels left out of her father's love. "I am, like, seriously, love me more!" Outside of the fact that Elizabeth wants more direct attention from George, she feels that life is decent around her Dad. They eat at five-star restaurants all the time, and they are driven to school by George's limousine driver. While her young brothers love this life of wealth, Elizabeth prefers the simpler life with her Mom.

Chapter 2

Drama

Elizabeth keeps to herself most times during the school day, but she has occasions to go to her locker between classes to exchange books. Normally, this is an uneventful process, but one particular day, she is looking for her Chemistry book, so she stays at the locker longer than usual.

She is startled by a loud noise behind her, which turns out to be a quiet kid who sits in the front of their classroom. Elizabeth knows of him but doesn't talk to him. Actually, he doesn't talk to many people, but keeps to himself. He's exactly the kind of kid who bullies love to tease. When Elizabeth turns away from her locker, she sees that somebody knocked all the books out of this kid's hand, and he is standing with his hands raised. He is very pale and almost in tears.

Elizabeth looks from this scared kid to the bully who threw the books down. The bully's name is Hannah, and her boyfriend, Ethan is there supporting her. Behind them is a small group of guys who all played different sports, and athletes tend to stick together, regardless of the ethical or moral implications of their collective actions. In short, it looked like Ethan, and therefore Hannah had a kind of "posse" that made them feel emboldened as bullies.

Elizabeth stares at Hannah, who knocked the books down. She's the girl with whom Elizabeth was close friends in early middle school. Back then Hannah wasn't mean, at least not overtly nasty in front of others. But something was always off about her.

It's very possible that Hannah was always going to become mean-spirited and feel entitled to push everyone around because her Mom was on the Board of Education. Everybody knew Hannah was spoiled a lot by her Mom, who had a reputation for being negative from the first day she took office during Hannah's middle school years. She was the kind of woman who felt validated by a title, and so becoming a member of the School Board certainly made her important.

Hannah's Mom was well known for threatening to take away children's recess or tell Santa to put them on the "naughty list" in order to get what she wanted. Occasionally, she went against the rest of the Board, but her overpowering voice caused them all to back down. Naturally, having a bully for a mother helped Hannah become one, and the worst thing you could do to Hannah's mom would be to call her daughter a "runt" or "bully." When Hannah was younger, she was the shortest girl in her class and was sick a lot, so the nickname "runt" kind of stuck.

In order to continue to protect Hannah in high school, and because she had quite a large ego, her mom had successfully run for the District School Board. So, all of the faculty and staff were afraid of her. If any student, faculty member, or Board member tried to enforce disciplinary actions against her precious Hannah, she would find some academic reason to judge them incompetent, and then push for them to be expelled or fired. Sadly, nine times out of ten she got what she wanted, and that person was gone within a month.

Well, there in the hallway stands Elizabeth, Hannah and boyfriend Ethan, and the nerd. By now, a crowd of students looking for a fight gathers around them, and no teacher has come from a classroom yet to tell everyone to move on to class. Elizabeth suddenly realizes she must take some action because everything is happening right next to her locker. She can't even get through the crowd to her next class without doing or saying something.

"Why don't you just leave him alone?" she says in a non-aggressive tone. Hannah most aggressively pushes

Ethan towards Elizabeth, as if pushing a male forward will intimidate Elizabeth. Elizabeth remembers him too. Back in middle school she liked him, but he wasn't into girls much. He was kind of a nerd. Anyways, she moved on to high school without him ever saying a word to her. Still, at this moment she feels she has some rapport with him because they came from the same middle school. She contemplates her next sentence carefully because everyone is watching.

Ethan remembers her from middle school too, and wants to respond in a non-threatening way, but when he sees the size of the crowd of their peers, he knows he must say something back with at least a little force. He also has Hannah standing slightly behind him and can feel her breath close to his upper arm. "Give me a reason why I should," he said responding to Elizabeth with an evil undertone.

Elizabeth is taken by surprise, but she's quick with her own retort: "You used to be a straight "A" student, and I'm sure you can come up with one by yourself." Ethan looks around with embarrassment as the group starts to giggle. Back in middle school he was a really hard-working kid and had amazing grades. He was even the Valedictorian for their graduating class. It was his intellect that attracted Elizabeth to him originally. But over the summer and freshman year he got bullied a lot from kids in his high school. They picked on him because he wore glasses, which did not help his cause. Therefore, his way of adjusting was to let his grades and glasses go, and to get in good with the popular athletes.

Ethan had become one of the most popular kids in the school and his friends were known for hurting other kids and picking fights randomly for no particular reason. By the middle of his sophomore year, he was the "leader of the pack." It was so bad that even seniors would run in order to avoid him. Today he decided to challenge a poor freshman who was just trying to take a few books from his locker.

"But ....", Ethan said in a nervous voice, not really wanting to insult Elizabeth.

Then Hannah stepped in front of him. *"Good for nothing,"* she said as she rolled her eyes turning towards

Elizabeth. "Look, Ethan, I saw this idiot messing with you, so I knocked his books down because I love you, Baby." Wow, Hannah's 4'11" frame seemed to stretch up to the height of those male athletes! Ethan did not really like the way she treated other people or the way she spoke, and he wasn't flattered by her saying she loved him. But like so many high school kids whose only desire is to fit in, Ethan had convinced himself that he must have this popular girl for his steady girlfriend. If he tried to oppose her for any reason, she would threaten to never talk to him again.

Ethan is literally "saved by the bell" because the late bell to class rang and everyone scattered to get to their respective classes before their teachers locked the doors and shut them out. So, just like that, the poor boy picks up his stuff and runs away, leaving Hannah, Ethan and Elizabeth staring at each other. Ethan and Elizabeth just want to get to class, so Ethan gently grabs Hannah's arm and escorts her away from Elizabeth by whispering sweet things in her ear. Her wrath has turned to giggles. Elizabeth literally runs to her class, almost sliding through

12

the door before her teacher steps past her to lock anyone else out for being late.

Elizabeth can't focus on her lesson because she is trying to process what just happened. How does she feel about Ethan after seeing him up close for the first time since middle school? She definitely has no happy feelings for Hannah, and if she were honest, she didn't care about that boy who was bullied. But she does have integrity and hates to see anyone bullied if she can do anything to diffuse a bad situation. Would she do the same thing again if it happened this way? She tells herself that she definitely would do the same thing. Now she can open her chemistry book and pay attention to the instructor.

Chapter 3
Betrayal

At Elizabeth's high school there are Saturday night dances every other month, and there is one coming up this Saturday night. About half the school shows up to this party because it's a good reason to hang out with friends and dance. They have some snacks and soft drinks, and the students treat it like a sort of date night event. In the town, there are some well-known local D. J.s, and it's always a surprise to see which one will be at the next dance. Of course, there's always the intrusion of chaperones, but the parents who chaperone are much more friendly than the teachers who constantly remind students of the consequences for "minor offenses."

The party starts off with Elizabeth coming in with her close friends. Because she's an introvert at heart, she sits in a corner and enjoys watching her fellow students dance. She pulls her best friend aside, wanting to tell her about her new and confusing feelings for Ethan since the day of the altercation in the hallway near her locker. Elizabeth always gives her friends and classmates second chances when they do something she feels is wrong.

The music is too loud for them to talk inside, so her best friend suggests that they go outside to talk. She is intrigued by Elizabeth saying she's confused about her feelings for Ethan. They go outside and find two chairs close to each other, not noticing that Hannah is also at the dance and also outside. For a brief moment, Elizabeth's best friend catches the eye of Hannah, and it's apparent that the two of them are friends. They give each other a quick smile, as the best friend turns towards Elizabeth, who is clueless that Hannah is there or that she is also friends with Hannah.

The best friend leans into Elizabeth and quietly says, "C'mon, girl, spill the tea!" Elizabeth begins by recounting the incident in the hallway where Hannah was needlessly bullying this boy while Ethan stood by without stopping her. Now Elizabeth knew how mean Hannah was to everyone, but she wanted to share how Ethan seemed to be uncomfortable as a bully. "I can't put my finger on it, but I felt in my heart that Ethan wasn't happy being Hannah's boyfriend. He knows better than to choose a mean girl for his girlfriend. I think I told you that I used to like him back in middle school, and now here we were in this situation where I got a glimpse of his heart. I wanted to talk some sense into him, and I believe he would have listened if not for Hannah breathing down his neck."

Elizabeth's best friend nodded in agreement, but said, "Are you saying that you want to see him again?"

Elizabeth's face got a little flushed with color, but she wasn't changing her mind. "When you wrinkle your nose like that, I can tell you don't like the idea of me wanting to have a relationship with someone I knew in middle school. But if I'm honest with myself, I have to say yes, I want to see him again. You're my best friend, so I know I can trust you to keep my secret. I don't know what I'll do next, but I will keep you posted, OK?"

Her best friend makes the sign across her body that means, "Cross my heart and hope to die." So, Elizabeth fells very comfortable that her friend would never reveal her secret, and both girls hug before returning to the dance. But just as her friend opens the door to the dance, she looks back at Elizabeth and says, almost in a whisper, "Watch your back." Elizabeth was a little confused, but she was certain that her friend could also be friends with Hannah and still not betray her confidence. She has nothing to worry about.

Within two days of this promise from Elizabeth's best friend, they are all in the cafeteria at the beginning of the lunch period. Hannah pulls a group of girls to a corner of the cafeteria, pressing Elizabeth's best friend to reveal what they were talking about in secret at the last

Saturday night dance. Hannah is pushy and persistent, looking from one girl to another. After some silence, Hannah reminded Elizabeth's best friend that she was also Hannah's friend. "Listen, you're my friend too, and if our friendship means anything to you, then you better tell me what's going on with Elizabeth. I know you know."

The friend feels nervous as she looks around the cafeteria to see Elizabeth going through the lunch line. Is Elizabeth reading her mind? Hannah says something loud and mean that causes her friend to look back at her. "It better not have nothing to do with my Ethan!"

Her friend feels helpless and trapped, since her secret does, in fact, directly relate to Ethan. She's gotta say something, as the other girls in the small cluster of ladies around her look directly at her. "You think everything's about you and Ethan. Well, everyone knows Elizabeth liked him in middle school, and I'm not sure but I think he liked her back."

"What did you just say?" screamed Hannah?

At that point it seemed that everyone in the whole cafeteria turned their attention to Hannah and her friends. But they quickly returned to their conversations, and Hannah lowered her voice. But before she could utter another word, Elizabeth's best friend interjected, "Wait! Wait a minute! I wasn't suggesting that they like each other now .... but .... what if they did?"

Hannah almost gets physical with her friend, as she tries to control her anger. Her friend quickly walks away, leaving Hannah and the other girls standing there in silence.

By now, Elizabeth is looking around the cafeteria for her friend, who is coming over with her lunch tray. They sit together, but her best friend nervously looks away. Elizabeth asks if everything is OK, to which her friend quickly says she's fine. On the other side of the cafeteria, Hannah has found Ethan and they are engaged in quiet, but purposeful conversation, complete with hand gestures, arms raised and a look of disgust on Hannah's face. In an instant, Hannah has grabbed Ethan's arm and is almost pulling him towards Elizabeth and her best friend.

Hannah has no time for pleasant talk. "Do you like MY boyfriend? What do you think you're doing anyway?"

Elizabeth and Ethan are both confused by Hannah's words, and Elizabeth gives an angry glance at her best friend, who is still looking away from her. Elizabeth looks from her friend to Hannah and then to Ethan. She decides to be bold and admit she does like him. But Ethan steps forward and speaks instead. "What if I do like her?"

With that, Ethan walks away as Hannah stands, red-faced and fighting back tears. Students at all the tables around Elizabeth's are now silent and listening to this conversation. Hannah begins to get red in the face, so she strikes out at individuals who are staring at her. "If I tell my Mom any of this, I can get you suspended for harassing me. I hear your giggling and snickering." Everyone looks away because they know Hannah's mother is as much of a bully as she is. Someone drops a fork, and the sound if it hitting the floor changes the focus of everyone, as Hannah storms out of the cafeteria.

Elizabeth's best friend now looks into her eyes and gives a look of sorrow. Elizabeth has too much integrity to confront her best friend with a bunch of students sitting around them, so she eats her lunch in silence. Her best friend does the same. They both know that Elizabeth is not in the head space to receive an apology, and her friend keeps changing words in her head about how she will express her deep regret for betraying her best friend. Lunch is over, and everyone must get to class.

Chapter 4
A Change in Tides

Elizabeth decides to remain calm and talk to her Mom about this betrayal that has really upset her. Mom says, "You're too naïve to trust your friend like that, and even believing that a guy like Ethan would honestly reveal that he has feelings for you. He was probably trying to get away from Hannah."

That feels like a punch to the gut for Elizabeth. She came to her mother for comfort and validation, and now she has doubts about the motives of Ethan, instead of getting advice about how to handle her best friend at school tomorrow. Elizabeth trusts that her Mom loves her and wouldn't hurt her. She's so confused, as she quietly returns to her bedroom to process everything that's happened today and tonight.

She hears her brothers talking outside her bedroom door, and she's in no mood for them to open it and say something stupid. But all of a sudden, she begins to think about her Dad, wondering if she should call him to discuss her problems. "No, he wouldn't understand me because he never understands me."

The next morning before school, Elizabeth sees Ethan walking from the bus stop towards the school, and she races in his direction but stops when she's close to him. After all, she doesn't want to appear desperate. "Hey … hi, Ethan. Um… what's up?" Immediately her face gets red because she regrets that clumsy greeting. "Hey, can we talk about what happened yesterday in the cafeteria?" Ethan nods in agreement. Elizabeth asks, "Did you mean what you said to Hannah about liking me?"

"Well, if I did mean it, would you say you liked me back?" The bell rang, startling both of them, as they rushed across the campus to get to class on time.

During the beginning of gym class, Elizabeth and her best friend are in the locker room changing into the unfashionable gym uniforms. The friend says straight up, "I can't tell you how sorry I am that I jeopardized our friendship by falling into Hannah's trap. She set me up." Elizabeth wants to move past this and stay best friends, so she gives a look of compassion and forgiveness.

Just then, Hannah, who must have heard her name spoken, comes over to announce that Elizabeth can have Ethan. "But don't think I'm going away anytime soon. I decided before yesterday to quit Ethan, so you haven't won any victory. You'll be miserable with him anyway, while I move on to better things." With that said, everyone makes their way to gym class.

The guys and the girls like to play around during gym class. The teacher announces that everyone will jog around the track three times to warm up. Elizabeth and Ethan start out jogging in separate clusters of students, but by the second lap, they are jogging at the same pace. She makes small talk, and then Ethan reminds her that she

24

never answered his question earlier in the day. "You didn't answer my question either and I asked mine first."

Ethan tries to downplay how much he likes Elizabeth. "OK, I guess you're cute – well pretty. I might … I mean I would go out with you."

With that, Elizabeth accelerates her pace and jogs ahead of Ethan. Although he is very athletic, he slows down to allow her to move a distance from him. He can't see Elizabeth's big grin, since he just said what she had wanted to hear. Gym class ended and everyone ran to get to the next class.

The next period was the only other class they shared together, which was Life Skills. While the teacher was getting prepared to begin the lesson, Elizabeth brings up the conversation where she first saw Ethan with Hannah, who had just knocked the books out of a defenseless student's hands. Embarrassed, but not yet ready to abandon his tough attitude, Ethan begins to raise his voice in defense of his actions. He catches himself and slows his conversation to agree with her assessment of the bullying situation.

Elizabeth reminds him of how really caring and smart he used to be in middle school, and she appeals to him to go back to being that person. Throughout the lesson, Ethan hears Elizabeth's voice in is head and tells himself he really should change. Yes, deep down inside him, he wants to be that smart and caring friend and student everyone respected. He doesn't have to be a bully or be with one in order to get respect. He decides to write out a plan to get back on track academically, and he feels that Elizabeth will be happy with the "new Ethan."

Right after school, Ethan's buddies approach him to do something really juvenile and stupid, not knowing that Ethan has had a change of heart. They are giggling with excitement over what they're about to do, and for the first time, Ethan realizes that he doesn't want any part of this anymore. When they see his facial expression showing doubt about joining them, one of his friends mocks Elizabeth's walk and talk, challenging Ethan by saying, "Is Elizabeth the girl you dumped Hannah for? Hannah was so much better for you, and we don't know what you see in Elizabeth. She's a nerd and isn't even as pretty as Hannah, who's perfect for you. And remember you'll never get in trouble because her mother is on the Board of Education. What's Elizabeth got to offer?"

He responds to the question about what Elizabeth has to offer. "What do you guys have to offer me?" They are stunned and can't respond right away. Ethan walks away from them slowly, but everyone knows their relationship has changed forever. He's now motivated to pull up his grades and join Elizabeth as an Honor Roll student thinking about college.

While the guys were having this conversation, Elizabeth's best friend is standing nearby and overhears the whole thing. She can't wait to redeem herself in her best friend's eyes, so she texts her, but Elizabeth doesn't answer because she is in an after-school club meeting in the library. Her friend can hardly contain her excitement, so she runs across campus to the library. By the time the meeting ends, she has caught her breath, and grabs Elizabeth's arm to pull her around the corner for privacy.

"Girl, did you hear what Ethan did for you today?" Elizabeth makes a confused sound, but her friend interrupts her. "Ethan stood up to all the guys for you and told everyone he wanted to be with you – just you!"

Elizabeth doesn't want to allow her heart to be broken, and yet she wants to believe what her best friend is saying. "You can't be serious!"

Her friend says, "Don't take my word. Call Ethan and just say hello. I will bet he'll tell you what I'm saying now."

Chapter 5
Be You!

Elizabeth quickly curled her hair and put on just a little makeup and some nude color lipstick that made her lips shine. She closed her bedroom door for maximum privacy from her pesty little brothers and took a deep breath before calling Ethan to Facetime him. She didn't have something prepared to say but trusted her instincts that the right words would come out.

Ethan is unsure of the reason for Elizabeth's call, but he sees that she is Facetiming him, so he answers with his phone camera pointed towards the ceiling. Elizabeth speaks first. "Hey, my friend told me that you were with the guys, and they tried to get you to go and do something that could have gotten you into trouble. They said some unflattering things about me, too, but you stood up for me. Is that true?"

He admitted that he stood up for her and he was not sorry about it. "I don't have anything to do tonight, so do you want to hang out?" Now his phone camera was pointed to their two faces, and both of them smiled. They agreed to meet in half an hour at the ice cream place.

As they stood in the line, Ethan said, "I think I remember that back in middle school your favorite ice cream was butter pecan. Am I right?"

"I'm impressed. It's not like we have ice cream at school, so you have a great memory," Elizabeth said with a light chuckle.

At first, they sat in silence, enjoying the ice cream. Ethan's mind was full of regrets. He told himself that he never wanted to be a bully or to pick on helpless kids at school. He actually hated being with Hannah, and really didn't like her mother. He was sorry he had lost sight of his goals and decided to hang out instead of getting good grades. Deep down, he always wanted to know Elizabeth better, and here he was having ice cream with the young lady who made him happy.

Meanwhile, Elizabeth was thinking how she used to like Ethan, but didn't like the guy he had become with his bully friends. She thought Hannah was a terrible influence on Ethan, pushing him to do things that were against his nature. She was glad to see a visible change in his attitude.

Before they finished eating their ice cream cones, Ethan leaned in to be close to Elizabeth, and asked, "Would you be my lady?"

(Read a little about Abigail on the next page)

31

About the Author

I am seventeen years old, born in Maryland and living in Florida for six years. I am active in several sports, but basketball is my favorite. I'm not what you would consider tall, but I am working on stamina and speed. I'm great at shooting baskets.

I also love music, playing saxophone and piano. I sing sometimes too. I have been part of *Faith Works Drama* for a year, and we do general performances for live audiences. Musicals are so much fun.

So, You Want Your Name in Lights is a camp and organization that helps kids write their own music and meet others to showcase our talents. I was a finalist in the showcase last year and hope to win this year.

I have just written my first book! You can reach me for a book signing or a public speaking event at: **GivesJoy@gmail.com**

Made in the USA
Middletown, DE
24 May 2022